'Cos This Is How Villains Are Made

A. Carys

A. Carys

The characters and events portrayed in this book are fictitious. Any similarity to real persons, living or dead, is coincidental and not intended by the author.

No part of this book may be reproduced, or stored in a retrieval system, or transmitted in any form or by any means, electronic, mechanical, photocopying, recording, or otherwise, without express written permission of the publisher.

Copyright © 2024 A. Carys

All rights reserved.

'Cos This Is How Villains Are Made

BOOKS IN THIS SERIES

Of Doors and Betrayal

The Pickpocket and the Princess

The Master, My Wings, Our Service

'Cos This Is How Villains Are Made

A Circus of Wonder

A Sentence to Death

A Deal With The Devil

Let Her Go

The Three

Queen Rory, The Banished

A. Carys

'Cos This Is How Villains Are Made

DEDICATION

I tried to curl my hair, now I look like I've been electrocuted.

A. Carys

'Cos This Is How Villains Are Made

CHAPTER ONE

I love walking the palace grounds.

The whole place is beautiful. Roses, lavender, astilbe, begonias, coneflowers, marigolds and tulips bloom within the tidily kept beds. Beautiful white bricks outline each bed, each and every one looking as pristine as the day they were put in. Purple slates make up the garden paths, and they crunch nicely underneath my boot as I walk over them. I do a small jump, landing back on the slates with a satisfying crunch.

"When are you going to stop doing that?" my half-brother, Kai, asks while laughing.

"The day you stop letting me walk with you on your lunch break."

"That'll never happen. Spending my lunch break

with you is the only option," he says with sarcasm lacing his tone.

I roll my eyes playfully, knowing that he isn't wrong about his lunch break being the only option. Well, technically it's not the only option, but his work hours are crazy, especially since he's juggling two jobs which means he doesn't get back to the cottage as often as he would like.

Kai worked hard for so many years in order to earn the positions he has within the royal household. He serves as both the Chief and Personal Guard for the twin princes, so he's always busy. His lunch hour has become our golden time. I come up from the cottage he brought for me on the outskirts of town, in the Flower District of the island, and we sit in the palace meadows. I always bring a picnic basket filled with enough cheese and cucumber sandwiches to feed at least four people. I also bring a soft blanket and two glass cups, while Kai brings a pitcher of the palace's finest cranberry juice.

"So, how's Meika?" I ask as I lay the blanket on the freshly cut grass.

"She's good. She's very busy at the moment as

the princes have her doing some kind of heavy research project. Whenever I see her she's always buried beneath a pile of books."

Meika works as the princes' assistant, working to their every beck and call. Fetching items that are meant to be hard to procure, reading articles, and annotating books that will help the princes' further their knowledge before their coronation. She's a lovely girl, and despite my best efforts, neither she nor Kai seem to recognize that they like each other.

"What kind of research?" I take a bite of one of the sandwiches.

"No idea. Wish I did though, maybe then I could offer to help her."

I stare at him, resting one hand on my hip. "And when would you find the time to help her? During lunch?"

He shakes his head, smiling cheekily. "Of course not. I'd do it during the night shifts. I don't have a lot to do when the princes are asleep, so I could read stuff for her, take notes on what I think might be important."

"Aww, you're blushing," I say teasingly.

"Shut up," he mumbles as he shoves one of the tiny triangle sandwiches into his mouth.

I laugh. "On a serious note though, I'm glad you're happy."

"Thanks, sis."

We eat in silence, just enjoying each other's company. The hour always passes quickly, and each time I wish he had a longer break. I wish we could spend more time together.

"How are the Blocking Beads? Are they working?" he asks lowly, his eyes darting around the meadow.

I nod. "They're working fine. The tattoos are invisible whenever I wear them."

Blocking Beads. Beads that can make inherited, DNA specific markers, disappear. They're extremely hard to get hold of, but by some miracle, Kai managed to find me eight bracelets worth of them. Four per wrist to give me the strongest dose of their power. I use them to hide the silver tattoos that spiral from my collarbones, down and around my arms, before finishing at the tips of my fingers. It's a symbol of an ancient bloodline, the Eilin line.

'Cos This Is How Villains Are Made

People with Eilin blood are healers. They have the ability to heal anything from paper cuts and skinned knees to near fatal wounds and diseases. Eilin's were worshipped for years; they were highly praised and placed upon pedestals. That was until a scientist discovered something unique about an Eilin's blood. The scientist discovered that if someone was able to get their hands on, at least, three vials of Eilin blood, they'd be able to control the Eilin that it was taken from. This quickly became a problem, and a barrage of attacks began, with mortals desperate to get their hands on Eilin blood. The attacks turned into a full scale war led by the Royal Family. The Royals wanted as many Eilin's under their control as possible, but the people revolted, claiming that they were just as entitled to an Eilin's blood as the Royals were. Eventually, the war reached a point where it was believed that all Eilin were dead, which they mostly were. The war had taken such a toll on the Eilin bodies that they were dying within a few days of being captured. It was, essentially, a massacre.

Fortunately though, for two female Eilin elders, they discovered the first Blocking Beads. They used them to cover their tattoos and survive for another 40 years after the war ended. They wrote books about the Beads; about experiments they'd tried with both the Beads and the Eilin blood. They left the books for future Eilin, in the hopes that one day there would be more. The women went on to live full lives, both marrying gentle men who took great care of them. Both elders had one child, one girl and one boy. That girl, the child who would inherit the Eilin DNA, would turn out to be my grandmother. My grandmother didn't possess the ability to heal, and neither did my mother when she was born. That led my grandmother to believe that the Eilin were officially extinct.

And they were, until I was born. Five pounds 4 ounces, a head full of tight ginger curls and bright silver tattoos. Thankfully, it was a home birth, away from nurses at the local hospital. My mother and grandmother kept me hidden, protected, for 17 years. But they weren't alone in that. Six years before I was born, my mother gave birth to Kai. She didn't stay with Kai's dad though, they never married but ended up sharing custody of Kai. Then when I was born and my father was nowhere to be found, my mother sought out Kai's father, a man named Dane. Once my mother explained what had happened, Dane married my mother and together, along with my grandmother, kept me hidden. It wasn't until Kai gifted me the Blocking Beads on my 25th birthday that I was finally able to venture out of the cottage.

"Good. Never take them off until you're about to go to sleep. And make sure you wear them when you go out, especially when you're here."

"I know, Kai, I know. Mum and Dane told me about the Blocking Beads all the time."

"I know they did, but they're not here anymore. It's just you and me, and I'm doing all I can to protect you." He pauses and I watch his throat work. "I don't want to lose you."

"You won't lose me. I know you're just trying to protect me and I'm beyond grateful for that. You're my rock, Kai, and I wouldn't be sitting in this meadow if it wasn't for you. But I can't do anything with my life and that thought always gets to me. I can't work because that would mean taking off my bracelets. I can't date because if they stay over then they might see my tattoos because the bracelets aren't comfortable to sleep in. I can't trust anyone except for you, and I have no friends. I'll live a long life, one that will potentially outlast yours and your children's children. And for all of that time, I will be alone."

"I know. I'm working on it though. I'm trying to find more practical ways to help you live a normal life. I *want* you to have a normal life. We'll get through this, together," he says, grabbing my hand and squeezing it.

I nod, smiling at him. "Together."

"Has the team found out anything else? Any clues as to who is attacking people?"

I shake my head. "Nothing yet, but there's something odd about the attacks."

"What do you mean?"

"I was with Shepherd the other day; he was letting me look at the most recent victims and I have reason to believe that this is blood induced. They both had varying attack patterns, definitely done with the same weapon, but it's got to be different people. Shepherd was saying that the way the wounds were made would suggest that the attacker, or attackers, were different heights and weights. I didn't say anything to him, obviously, but I think someone could be using blood to influence people to kill others," I say to him.

"Could there be more like you?"

"No, not in the Eilin sense at least. I'm still me, the only one, but in the books I found there were suggestions that there could be a mutation in the Eilin line. It was unlikely to happen, something rare that would develop over a long period of time. The books also said that the mutated line would do the opposite of healing. It kills, but not before poisoning the mind of the person infected. It can also be used for control so it would explain a lot, I just don't know how it's being used against people. Our grandmother did the tests and research so I'm sure it–"

"Kai, who is this lovely lady?"

CHAPTER TWO

I freeze.

I don't recognise the voice, but the look on Kai's face suggests we might be in trouble.

"Your Highness, this is my half-sister, Meredith," he says, getting up and bowing. He offers me his hand and I scramble to my feet.

"Your Highness," I say as I curtsey clumsily.

"Please, call me Brandon."

"It's a pleasure to meet you, Brandon."

He smiles. "The pleasure is all mine, Meredith."

"Please, call me Merry."

"Well, it's a pleasure all the same. Kai, my brother is waiting for you, he'd like to take a walk to the cemetery."

"Of course Your Highness," Kai says. I hear him

take a few steps and then he appears in front of me. "Can you make it back to the cottage by yourself?"

"No need to worry Kai. I can look after Miss Merry until you return."

"You okay with that?" Kai asks as he stares at me.

"Yeah, it's fine. I'm fine, go," I murmur. He nods before walking off in the direction of the other prince, the one I first saw out of the corner of my eye.

We stand in silence until both Kai and the prince disappear from sight.

"So, Miss Merry, tell me about yourself," Brandon says as he outstretches his hand to me. I hesitate for a moment before placing my hand in his. He pulls me closer, so that I'm standing next to him, our arms brushing against each other.

"My blanket, the lun–" His finger gently pressing against my lips has me stopping halfway through my sentence.

"I will have someone come and pack everything away. It'll be ready for you to collect when you leave, okay?"

I nod, more than just slightly stunned at the man

before him. I'd heard the rumours. People always describe Prince Brandon as having the deepest voice, that even when he whispers, people flock to obey the words that fall from his mouth. I didn't quite believe that it was something that actually happened, but I'll be damned if I don't believe them now.

"Now, about yourself?"

I recover, taking a breath and clearing my throat. "What would you like to know?"

"How old are you?"

"25. You?"

"28. What do you do for work?"

"At the moment I'm part of an agency that supports the families and those close to the victims of the recent attacks that have been happening around the island." I leave out the part where I'm independently investigating the cases, he doesn't need to know that.

"Interesting. I've heard of those attacks, and I'm sorry that my soon to be subjects are going through that. Is there anything you think I could do to help?"

I'm taken aback by the question. But involving one of the princes in my work would cause chaos.

And my preliminary investigations are showing links to the Royal Hunters from the war, but I've no concrete evidence to suggest that anyone in the Royal Family is involved. At the moment.

"Not really, at the moment it's up to the detective team in charge of the case and my team aren't detectives. We just support those affected."

He nods in response.

We continue talking, chatting about anything and everything under the sun.

Do you have any other siblings? *No, just Kai.*

Are you ready to be coronated? *Yes, but I've still got some nerves buzzing under my skin with worry.*

Do you see Kai a lot? *We have lunch together most days, since he took the promotion he doesn't come home much.*

Do you mind that you and your brother are going to have to share the throne? *Not at all, I think it's better that there's two of us. We can work together to better the lives of our people, feed off each other's ideas and come up with the best ways to support our subjects.*

Brandon guides me through the rest of the

meadow. He doesn't seem to mind as I stop to smell every different flower we come across. In fact, while I admire the flowers, he explains what they are. I feel a childish, giddy joy bubble up inside of me as I get to know the flowers I've sat next to almost daily. When we reach the edge of the meadow, Brandon takes my hand and pulls me over to the sacred willow tree. The willow tree is at the back of the palace grounds and is connected to the Silver Lake. I've only seen it from a distance a handful of times but being able to see it up close is everything I thought it would be. The branches of the willow tree cascade down like a waterfall. Vibrant, light green leaves gently brush together in the breeze, and a dusting of pollen and dandelion seeds swirl in the air. It's magical, and the world turns silent the second Brandon brushes the branches out of the way and guides me inside. We stand inside the willow branches, in a space so tranquil and beautiful.

"It's beautiful," I say, slowly twirling as I look up at the trunk of the tree.

"It is."

"Thank you for showing me this." I smile at him,

finally dragging my attention away from the tree.

He smiles and shoves his hands in his pockets. "The pleasure is all mine. I'm glad to see someone so enthusiastic about it. Not many people truly appreciate the beauty of nature."

"Kai and I choose to eat in the meadow because nature was a big part of our childhood. The cottage we lived in when we were children, and the cottage I live in now, are surrounded by dense forest and stone walls covered in ivy and wildflowers."

"Kai doesn't talk about his childhood often. And he didn't mention he had such an intriguing sister."

"You find me intriguing?" I ask, crossing my hands over my chest.

He nods. "There's something different about you, Merry. You're normal, but at the same time I don't think you are. Do you have a lot of secrets, Merry?" Brandon asks nonchalantly, like it's possible he didn't just deduce my entire life and brain in one sentence.

"What?" I choke out, taking a step back.

Brandon seems to realise what he said as his face turns from inquisitive to shocked. "I'm sorry, Merry, that was completely inappropriate of me. I apologise."

I give him a small smile. "It's okay," I say, not being entirely sure how to salvage the calm and comfortable atmosphere we had.

"It's not. I shouldn't have said those thoughts out loud, let alone have been thinking them."

"Brandon, it's fine, I'm fine. Let's just pretend it didn't happen." I feel bad for the guy, he looks genuinely upset about saying those thoughts aloud. I step toward him and carefully take his hand in mine. I gently squeeze his hand, letting him know that I'm not mad or upset at him.

He smiles at me appreciatively. "In a few days, there's going to be a Pre–Coronation Ball. I don't normally bring a guest but after letting my mouth do the work instead of my brain…"

"You want me to go with you?" I finish for him as I remove my hand from his.

He smiles. "Yes. Would you, Merry, go to the Ball with me?"

I smile at him. "I would love to," I beam, excitement bubbling inside of me at the thought of going to a Ball. "What's the dress code?"

"It's a masked ball, so a mask and a lovely dress.

'Cos This Is How Villains Are Made

Both of which I will give to your brother."

I nod, smiling. "Thank you. I guess I'll see you then."

"Well, you don't need to leave right now, how about I take you on a tour of the palace?"

"Okay, sure." I smile at him as I place my hands in the pockets of my skirt. "Lead the way."

CHAPTER THREE

In the 48 hours since meeting Prince Brandon, I've found several leads that might help the detective solve the murders that keep happening. I'm still undecided about when I will go to the detective with my findings, but I will. Eventually. It's important that she get justice for both the victims and their families.

The first lead I found was related to the blood being found on the victim. And no, this blood wasn't theirs. The blood found in the most recent victim had been significantly modified compared to a blood sample taken two years prior during his annual check-up. There were molecules that aren't recognisable as 'normal', and they indicate that the DNA being held in this blood was given to the victim via a blood swap or transfusion. The swap slash transfusion may have

'Cos This Is How Villains Are Made

happened by the perpetrator connecting an already open wound against a wound they created on the victim. But I don't believe it was meant to be a blood swap slash transfusion in the way I was originally thinking. I think that the perpetrator is connected to the mutated Eilin blood. The deadly, killing kind that could be used to poison and control someone.

Unfortunately, it's not something I can just bring up with the detective because I don't know if I can trust her. I can't know for sure that she wouldn't get curious about my extensive knowledge of blood, the gene mutations and a part of the island's history that happened well before I was born. I'd also have to be careful talking to her about it in the Detective's Station since that place is full of leaks. Nowhere on this island is safe to talk about anything secret, everything gets out eventually and that is scary to think about.

The second lead is in relation to the Royal Family. Back in the war, the Royals were known for having Jade cut weaponry. The Jade weapons were notoriously sharp and could inflict a lot of damage in a single swipe. The blades not only left a very specific cut on the person it was used against, but they also left traces of Jadeite, and Jadeite is a pyroxene mineral made of sodium and aluminium. So going by the fact that the tests run on the body showed very faint traces of Jadeite along the wound's edge, it would suggest that the Royals could somehow be involved in all of this. But that is more of a theory instead of a lead in the sense that those Jade weapons could be anywhere on the island. After the war, the palace was robbed and a number of Jade weapons were stolen, presumably sold on both the black and inter-universal markets. So the likelihood of someone else having a Jade weapon to hand is high, and that makes working out who is attacking these people even harder.

"Meredith?" Kai calls out, bringing me out of my thoughts. I leave my papers and test results on the table and rush to the front door.

I twist the key in the lock and open it, letting him in. "How long were you out there for?"

"A few minutes. What the hell were you doing?"

"Working. I think I've made some progress on the attacks."

"That's great, congratulations," he says as I

follow him through the cottage until he places down the box in his arms.

"What's in there?"

"A dress. And a mask. From *Brandon*," he says, putting emphasis on Brandon's name.

I smile, reaching for the box. I pull open the lid and find the most beautiful black fabric. I carefully remove the dress from the box and am instantly taken back by the beauty of it. A black, sleeveless corset is attached to a stunning skirt. Red thread accents the black fabric, running up from the hem of the skirt like veins. There's a thin, outer lining of shimmery fabric and it sparkles when the low sun rays streaming in through the window catch it. I take a peek at the mask and see the same black material with red detailing. This outfit is to die for.

"It's a nice outfit, but since when did you show interest in going to a ball hosted by the Royal Family?"

"I'm not, not really. Brandon invited me."

Kai's eyes widen. "Brandon invited you?"

"Uh-huh. When you had to go with Prince Liam, Brandon and I walked, and we talked. It got a little bit awkward, and then he invited me to the Ball."

He squints, looking suspicious. "I don't think it's a good idea."

"Why not?" I ask with a tilt of my head.

"There's something going on, and I don't just mean with the attacks."

"What kind of thing?"

"I'm not sure, but Meika was saying that Brandon has started showing interest in the attacks. And the research he has her doing has her feeling concerned. There's something going on."

"Maybe there is something going on with the coronation. Everyone is a bit on edge right now," I say, trying to reason with him.

He shakes his head. "Merry, this isn't like you. You're normally a lot more suspicious. Doesn't any of what I said strike you as odd?"

I huff. "Kai, this whole thing is odd. These attacks, the sudden death of the King and the coronation of the twin princes. It does strike me as odd, yes, but the oddest thing is being asked to a Ball by a prince. Yes, I'm suspicious, but that doesn't mean I'm not allowed to enjoy something like this."

"You need to stay safe, and as hidden as possible without becoming an outcast from society."

"I will. I promise you, that if things get even the slightest bit out of hand, I'll leave. I'll disappear and never see Brandon again. I'm not trying to be careless; I just want one night. One night of being normal and then I'll go back to hiding. To living my quiet little life and having picnics with you every day."

"I know you would. But I just want you to be careful, that's all. Extra vigilant because tensions are high, and the last thing you need is people coming for you because of your blood."

"I know. I'll be careful, especially with you as my escort?" I try, adding in my question right at the end.

"I'll be on the princes' detail the whole night."

"But if I'm with Brandon, then you'll be close by, right?"

"I guess so."

I step toward him and wrap my arms around his waist. "Everything'll be okay. *I'll* be okay. It's just one night of fun, what could go wrong?" I say rhetorically.

He sighs and returns the hug. "Everything could go wrong," he mumbles.

"Shut up."

CHAPTER FOUR

Everything on the island is quiet in the 24 hours leading up to the Ball. A little too quiet if you ask me. Attacks were frequent, happening every two to three days. But nothing has happened for four days.

"Are you sure there haven't been any more attacks?" Kai asks as he laces the back of the corset.

"I'm sure. I spoke to the detective, and she assured me that there haven't been any new attacks. At least, none that anyone has found."

"Please tell me that strikes you as odd."

"It does, and trust me, I'm just as confused as you are. The only reason I can think of is that it's going to happen tonight. It could happen at the palace, or the victim could be someone from the Ball and the perpetrator will be waiting for them to head home."

"All laced," he murmurs before handing me my mask. "But isn't that too obvious? Surely the person committing these murders would know that the people investigating would be expecting the attack?"

I shrug as I tie the mask securely behind my head. "You'd think they would, but these attacks are impulsive. They're messy and weird, so I wouldn't expect that the person, or people, behind this are properly in control of what they're doing."

"You think there might be multiple people behind this?"

I shrug again. "I've no idea, I've just been reading the reports and tests on the victims. If the attacks are every two to three days, and for arguments sake we say that it's just one person, it's clear they may need time to recuperate. That then leads to the thought that, if they do need time to recuperate, what is the length of time they need to be able to get back to full strength? And if that time is more than three days, does that mean multiple people are involved?"

"Your brain is fascinating. It's surprising the detective doesn't want your help."

"It's not that she doesn't want my help, it's that I

don't know if I can trust her. I've got to be careful and really think about when I reveal my independent investigation. Once I've sorted it and I'm confident in my work, I'll go to the detective," I say to him, hoping it comes across similar to that of a closing statement.

I slip into the only pair of casual boots I own before putting on the black shawl that was neatly tucked at the bottom of the box.

"Ready?" Kai asks.

"Yes, let's go."

※

I've never seen the palace so vibrant and lively. Even before the sudden death of the King, the palace was pale and grey. No obvious light could be seen from the outside. But tonight, the palace is lit up with candles and the experimental gas lamps. Cloth banners hang down from the top balcony and I can hear the band from out here.

Excitement bubbles within me. I've never been to anything like this, hell, I've never even *seen* anything like this before.

Kai escorts me to the carpet that has been laid

out. I show my invitation to the guard while Kai shows his credentials. The guards are satisfied and open the rope gate, ushering us both through. The guard whispers something into Kai's ear which has him straightening himself and nodding. His once calm demeanour has changed to a tight, worried expression.

"Is everything okay?" I ask as I follow close to him.

He hesitates as he looks at me. "I think so. Just, follow close to me and don't wander off until we find Brandon."

I nod, slightly worried about the sudden panic filling his voice. We walk along the carpet, and instead of heading straight inside, we detour around the side of the palace. We walk for no longer than a minute before I spot Brandon.

"Your Highness," Kai calls as we get closer to him.

Brandon turns to us. "Kai, thank god," he says, taking the steps two at a time. I try to follow Kai down the steps to see what Brandon and two others were looking at, but Brandon catches me around the waist. He pulls me into him so that I can't go anywhere.

"Brandon, let me go. I want to see what's going on."

"Trust me, Merry, you don't want to see that."

You don't want to see that.

Translation: there's a body.

"Is there a body down there?"

Brandon's silence is all the confirmation I need.

"Brandon, let me see it. I work with the agency supporting those affected by the attacks. Let me help."

He shakes his head. "You don't want to see it, sweetheart, it's bad."

I'm about to say something else when Kai comes back over. He stares at me.

"Tell me," I demand.

"I think it's another attack, but I'd need you to confirm it," he says, looking annoyed at the way Brandon is holding me.

I quickly peel myself out of Brandon's arms and head straight over to where everyone had been looking. Kai and Brandon follow me closely. Nausea settles in my stomach as I look at the body. It's definitely an attack. I carefully kneel down next to the body, getting closer so that I can examine it. I glance over the wounds and take note of the same jagged edges. The same kind of edges as the previous victims.

"Kai, do you have your notepad on you?"

He hands me the notepad and pen he normally carries on him. I started scribbling down my notes. *Jagged cuts. Faint traces and tiny spots of what could be Jadeite from the Jade weapons.* The other *blood surrounding the wounds, the little traces of black inside the smears.*

I note all of it down on a page from the notebook, taking down as much detail as possible before closing the pad and handing it back to Kai.

"Could you help me up please?" I ask, discovering that the lovely outfit I'm wearing is slightly restrictive when it comes to bending down.

Both men grab my arms and pull me up. I smile at them and smooth down the fabric of the skirt. I give the pen back to Kai.

"Kai, I need you to get the detective here, have her keep everything under wraps and give her my notes. It's important she gets them in case someone tries to tamper with the scene."

"Got it. Will you be okay, Your Highness?"

Brandon nods. "Yes, go and get this sorted. Don't let anyone else near here other than the Detective Turner."

"Yes sir."

Brandon starts to guide me away, but I struggle to pull my eyes away from the scene. Kai was right, there hadn't been any attacks over the last few days because it was going to happen tonight.

"So, your work is a little more involved than just *helping* the families."

I smile meekly. "Sort of. I'm not officially on the investigating team, but I'm putting together some good leads. It's a bit like a puzzle, and I like to think I'm pretty good at solving puzzles."

He nods. "Now, how about we leave the thoughts of death and mutilated corpses out here and go enjoy the night?"

I smile at him, placing my hand in the now extended one. "That sounds like a fantastic idea."

CHAPTER FIVE

Everyone inside the ballroom is completely unaware of what's happening outside right now.

The band is keeping everyone occupied, playing song after song. There've been group dances and circus entertainment to keep the guests happy. There's also flutes of wine floating around with the wait staff to keep most of the guests tipsy enough that they don't want to escape to the gardens where the detective is now looking after the scene of the attack.

Brandon hasn't left my side once. We've danced, we've laughed, and we've had awkward conversations with drunk politicians. Now, we're drinking the finest pressed apple and pear juice. It's something only the Royals can afford, and I have to admit to Brandon that I've not heard of pears before.

Apples, yes, but never pears.

"Where do you get this?" I ask as I take another sip from the glass flute.

"Imported. Can't get the stuff here because our climate isn't right for pears, hell, our soil isn't right for a lot of otherworldly fruit."

I sputter and cough. "Pears are from another world?"

"Yes. Quite a nice world too. Very modern and much more advanced than we are."

"Have you been?"

He shakes his head. "My father used to let Liam and I watch the exchange. At some point we might need to look into doing another. We seem to be running low on pears and other bits."

"That's so cool. And I'm sorry about your father, nothing can prepare you for a death like that."

He smiles. "Thank you. It was sudden, but not unexpected."

We drink in silence, leaning up against the large pillars that surround the dance floor. I'm slightly leaning against his chest as one of his arms is wrapped loosely around my waist. There's something about him that is comforting, I don't meet a lot of people for fear of them finding out about my tattoos. But Brandon feels familiar, comforting even. And while I know that should render me suspicious, it feels nice to finally get to know someone new. Someone who could be a friend, or even more if our fates take us in that direction.

"Thank you for my outfit, by the way. It's lovely," I say, breaking the silence.

"You're most welcome. I assumed that you liked the corset style since you were wearing one the day we met."

"I love that style. They're strangely comfortable." I glance down at what he is wearing. His black shirt stands out against a lot of the white shirts around the room, and the black trousers are hemmed with red patterning.

"We match," I say, smiling up at him.

"We do. I thought about making a statement so that everyone would know you are here with me and my brother. You're not for anyone else tonight, just us."

"That's mighty presumptuous of you. What

would have happened if I wanted to dance with others?"

"Then we would have cuffed you to our sides so that you couldn't leave."

I laugh. "Barbarian."

"Only for you," he says with a wink. I roll my eyes. Something about the way he said, *only for you*, has butterflies fluttering around my stomach. Any thoughts of just being friends with the princes' seem to have flown out of the window. And from the way Brandon has made clear that I am *theirs* tonight, I don't believe I will escape them any time soon, which means I will need to be careful with how this plays out. Because if I'm not careful and let this get out of control, it will only end badly for me.

"Brandon," says a guy as he steps closer to us.

"Liam. Everything sorted?"

Liam. Brandon's twin. And I mean twins in every sense of the word. Twins in the way they have their hair gently smoothed backwards. The way they both have a dimple on their left cheek when they smile and the fact that their eyes are the exact same deep shade of brown. And also that their suits are exactly the same. I almost struggle to tell them apart, except for the fact that Brandon is still leaning against the pillar.

"Yes. Kai has gone to see the detective, so I said I'd come and make sure that his sister was okay," he says, a little smirk playing at the corner of his lip.

"His sister is more than okay."

"It's nice to finally meet you. I'm Meredith, but you can call me Merry," I say, introducing myself after feeling more than a little offended by them talking about me as though I'm not standing in front of them.

"It's a pleasure, Merry. I've heard from my brother that you're quite an interesting girl."

I shrug. "I try to be."

"Well, how about a dance and we can get to know each other a little better?" Liam asks, stretching out his hand. I nod, taking his hand and let him pull me to the dance floor.

He instantly pulls me into hold, his grip on my waist leaves me tightly pressed against him. We start swaying before taking on steps that allow us to travel around the room. We spin and step and weave between the other couples on the dance floor.

We use the slower dances as a time to chat, to get to know each other decently well. I learn that he likes music. He can play the guitar and he sometimes sings. He has a soft spot for animals, and he loves to beat his brother at archery.

"You're quite the charmer, aren't you?" I say as he gently spins me outwards before pulling me back in.

"I try to be. But I have a feeling my brother has already staked a claim on you."

"I don't think so, and if he keeps saying that then I might have to cut off his fingers with said stake," I threaten, which makes him laugh.

"You're funny. Which is nice. It's different."

I tilt my head to the side. "How is it different?"

"Well, you're telling jokes. And threatening my brother's fingers rather than stroking my ego to try and show how marriage worthy you are."

"What is with you two and marriage?"

"It's a normal thing to think about, especially at the moment. But I mean it when I say you're different, Merry."

I roll my eyes. "That's ridiculous."

"It's not. You're refreshing and I really like that about you. I don't know if you would believe in something like love at first sight, but I think I feel something like that tonight, Merry."

I nod, feeling both flattered and slightly suspicious at the fact that both brothers seem to be very interested in marriage and love. "I'm not looking for love. But I think it's safe to say that I've gained two friends," I tell them, nipping the love at first sight issue in the bud. I'm not looking for love and I never will be. Unfortunately I can't just say that to them because they'll ask questions, so it's better if I stay in control of the situation. So means it'll be up to me to put an end to the odd friendship we've formed.

"Ouch. Just friends?"

"No. *Good* friends," I tease which makes him suddenly dip me to the point where one of my feet has actually left the ground.

"Take it back."

I laugh. "No."

"Take it back." He spins me while I'm dangling, and I squeal with laughter.

"Fine, fine. I take it back."

He brings me back up and supports me while all the blood rushes away from my head.

"Are you done yet?" Brandon asks as he comes towards us.

"Maybe," Liam says as he pulls me impossibly closer to him, so close that my hands are gripping the lapels of his blazer. I feel Bandon step close as well, my back resting against his chest. The two of them are mighty touchy and clingy tonight, Liam slightly more so.

"Right, ladies and gentlemen." Everyone turns to look at the bandstand. "It's been wonderful to play for you all, but as the night draws to a close we've saved our best for last. A nice and slow, romantic song for you all to dance with your loved ones to."

"May we both have this dance, Merry?" Brandon asks, but his tone implies that it wasn't actually a question.

I nod, knowing that I won't be able to escape them. "How does that work?" I ask as they both take hold of my hands.

"Just follow our lead."

The band starts playing as the three of us sway

gently. Both princes' hold one of my hands, and they take it in turns to spin round with me wrapped in their arms. It's quite simple actually, dancing with two people. As one spins me outwards, the other is ready to receive. It's slow and delicate but works in such a way that we seem to gather a crowd of hypnotised onlookers.

As the song starts to end, I close my eyes and just let the boys guide me. I let them manipulate me into dancing the way they want me to, and in that time, something clicks into place. Something heated and passionate shifts inside of me. I wonder if it has happened for the princes' as well. But as the feeling of serenity begins to fade, my tattoos start to burn. The burn runs along my arms and along my collar bones. It's painful and it feels as though it's trying to borrow under my skin.

My eyes pop open and I stare directly at Liam.

"You okay? What happened?"

Calm. I need to stay calm, so I gaze at my bracelets. One. Two. Three. Four. Five. Six. Seven. Eight. Eight bracelets means fully concealed tattoos.

I swallow. "Yeah, just warm. I think I drifted off

to another world," I say, trying to placate both them and myself.

"You looked happy, like you were floating away," Brandon says.

"Yeah, I think I was," I admit, looking between them as the music ends. Both my hands are entwined with theirs.

The light and floaty feeling returns, but it's joined by something else. Something that makes me feel like I'm in danger.

In danger of what though, I've no idea.

CHAPTER SIX

The detective has summoned me.

It's been two days since the Ball, and two days since the last attack. But news of the attack has been severely dampened by the gossip that's spreading. The gossip is about my dance with both princes at the end of the Ball. People who live near the cottage have been asking me to tell the story over and over, which I've been more than happy to do. Reliving the experience has my heart feeling warm and the butterflies fluttering in my stomach again.

The princes have taken over my thoughts, my every waking second. My stomach twists and flutters just at the thought of seeing them again. I fear it's becoming a problem. I can't allow myself to walk blindly into a friendship, or more as the princes like to remind me, with the family that hunted and killed mine just for their blood. Something about them has me never wanting to lose them, and that scares me. But I know I cannot let thoughts like that consume me, because if push comes to shove and I find myself in danger, then I'm going to have to leave. To go far away, to somewhere the princes will never find me.

I pull myself from my thoughts and finish getting ready to meet the detective. I head to the front door and grab my satchel before opening the door and leaving. I make sure to lock the door behind me before heading down the grassy path and through the canopy of trees. Once I reach the Detective's Station, I let myself in and ask the receptionist to let the detective know that I'm here for my appointment.

I take a seat in the waiting area. I pull the files out of my bag and flick back through the chunky stack of papers. Last night, the minute the summons game through the letterbox, I gathered up all of my papers, lab results, scene notes, victim connections, and so on, into a manila folder. I then shoved that into my bag and left it on the front door handle so that I wouldn't forget it.

"Detective Leigh Turner is waiting for you in room 5."

"Thank you." I get up and walk down the corridor.

When I reach room 5, I knock on the door frame. "Detective Turner?"

"Ah, hello," a feminine voice says. "You must be Meredith, come on in. Please, take a seat."

"Hi, yes. Lovely to meet you," I say as we shake hands. She closes the door as I take a seat at the desk in the middle of the room.

"Am I in trouble?" I question, slightly concerned since this room looks like the place criminals are questioned in.

"No, no, not at all. I just wanted to talk to you about the attack at the palace the other night."

"Did you get the notes that I took? My brother, Kai, should've given them to you."

She nods. "Yes, I got them, thank you. They were very helpful, especially since it rained moments before I arrived. It washed away a great deal of the blood that was left on the body which meant we couldn't take all the tests we wanted to."

"What rain?"

"There was a flash shower, it was over just as quickly as it began."

Damn it. "I know I'm not part of the investigation, but I've been looking at copies of all of the tests your team has been running, and I think I've found some links."

"Really? Wow, okay. Why don't you take me through your..." Detective Turner pauses momentarily. "Investigation."

I place the file in front of me. I open it and start to put the papers into their respective groups so that I can talk the detective through everything in chronological order.

I start with my theory about the weapon being used in every attack. I tell her that the blade was used by the Royal family during the war against the Eilin line. That it, not only, leaves traces of what it's made of, but also that it was used during the bloodletting rituals. The blade allowed the Royal family to harvest enough blood, cleanly and without contamination, in order to be able to take control of the person.

I tell her about the modifications that were

detected in the victim's blood, and how the modifications don't show up on tests that were on the person's medical history from years prior. I take her through the blood swapping process, and how I believe that the person might need time to recuperate after each attack. I also mention my theory about there being multiple people involved, potentially multiple attackers.

I finish by taking her through my theory about the person possibly being connected to the Royals. That the instability current flowing through the Royal household might have something to do with it, but I also let her know that that theory isn't as plausible as my first.

When I finish speaking, I take a breath and look at the detective. She looks stunned.

"That is something else. When your brother said that you were investigating, I didn't think he meant to this level."

"It's a case that is complex, it has tons of blood work and history that people might not know very well anymore."

She narrows her eyes at me. "History? As in the

Eilin History?"

I nod. "Yes."

"And you know a lot about this?"

"Yes. When my mother was alive she taught me about it, she was an Eilin carrier."

She nods. "And you? You know an awful lot, despite the teachings of your mother. It borders on experience."

I take a deep breath. "I do have experience dealing with Eilin, not only did I grow up around it, but I have practiced the Eilin ways." I take a deep breath as I mentally prepare myself for the risk I'm about to take. "What I'm about to show you must stay between us."

"What must stay between us?"

"This," I say as I roll off my bracelets and let my tattoos reveal themselves.

The detective looks stunned as her eyes glance over my tattoos. She blinks several times, and her mouth opens and closes as she tries to form words.

"I know it's a lot. I got involved because I know blood. I know the history of blood on this island, and I know how to work the stranger elements of this case."

"You wear Blocking Beads?" she questions.

"Yes. I'm the last one. I *will be* the last one. I'll live till I'm old and fragile, alone. I won't ever have kids because I won't risk giving this to anyone else." I pause for a moment as I pick up the first two bracelets for each wrist and slip them back on. "If you need help with the case, just let me know, I'm happy to offer my services."

The door to the room bursts open and both princes stumble in.

"Excuse me, Your Highnesses, this is a private meeting," yells Turner, pushing back from the table.

"We know, and we're sorry but we need to talk to Merry," Brandon says, and I'm frozen at the dishevelled appearance of both of them.

"You are aware this is a Detective Station? Where private and confidential conversations happen?"

"Yes, and again, we're very sorry but we really need to ask Merry something," Liam says, echoing his brother's words as he stumbles further into the room.

The detective sighs. "Fine. Five minutes and then Merry is coming to work with me."

Both princes' nod and scramble to grab chairs so that they can sit in front of me. They're smiling like idiots, and slightly freaking me out.

"What do you want? I'm a little busy."

"We wanted to ask," Brandon says as he looks at Liam.

Liam nods and finishes the question. "To ask if you'd go out with us. Like a date."

"A date?" I query.

"Yes. Like us meeting up, not tomorrow because we have meetings but the next day. In the evening, under the stars. The thing that couples do. A date. With us."

CHAPTER SEVEN

I'm stunned. Too stunned to even have a coherent thought run through my mind, so instead, I blurt out the first question that comes to my mind.

"You want me to go on a date? With *both* of you?"

"Yes. Is that a problem?"

I shake my head. "No, no. I just– I've not been on a date with one person, let alone two people before."

"We don't expect you to choose right away, or at all. But we want to test the waters if that's something you'd be willing try?" Liam questions as he shuffles to the edge of his seat.

I'm lost for words. Go on a date with both of them to then only choose one of them? *Or choose neither*, the rational part of my brain chips in.

"I– I'm lost for words."

"It's okay, we know we sprung this on you, but we felt that it was best to just say it. No beating around the bush or anything. If it doesn't work, it doesn't work and we can just be friends," says Liam as he takes my hand in his.

"Sure." I internally wince at my answer. *No*, I should've said no, but it's too late now and my mouth continues to work faster than my brain. "Why not test it. If not, like you say, we can be friends."

They both beam at my answer, taking hold of my hands and placing a kiss on the back of them. They smile at me before getting up from their seats.

"Meet us at the Rose Arch, we'll give Kai an outfit and then we'll take it from there. A slow, experimental date with no expectations."

I nod in agreement, smiling. "Well, the detective is waiting for me, so I'll see you soon."

The two of them get up and leave the room, leaving the door open so that the detective can come back in. As she does, I look down at my wrists and see that I've only got four bracelets on, two on each wrist, and my tattoos are partially visible.

Realisation dawns on me. My blood runs cold.

The princes' may have seen my tattoos.

I rush to put the rest of the bracelets on all the while silently berating myself for not putting them on quicker. The princes were the last people who I ever wanted to see my tattoos because they'd know exactly what they meant.

A knock on the door has me snapping my head up in a panic, thinking that they've come back to take me away. To take me to the palace and harvest my blood, but it's just the detective.

"That was unexpected," she says as she comes further into the room.

"It was. I don't even know how they knew I was going to be here," I say to her as I put on my final bracelet. My mind is racing, but the detective's presence comforts me slightly. I'm protected in here. I'm safe.

"Well, they're the princes, they can come and go as they please. Hard to say no to them."

"You got that right," I mumble as I pack away all of my papers into the folder.

"Well, I said that you'd be helping me on the case

after you'd finished with them. My team is waiting."

Excitement bubbles inside of me. "Really?"

"Yes. Your knowledge of blood and the history of everything is quite impressive. If we're going to have even the slightest bit of luck solving this then you're going to be an essential part of the team."

"Thank you. Can I just ask that we don't mention my tattoos? The last thing I want is more people knowing, and for my safety it's better if it stays between us."

"I have no interest in compromising your safety."

"Thank you."

"Right then, follow me," she says as she steps out into the door.

I scurry out of the room, following the detective down the hall and into the room where her team awaits.

※

Spending the entire day working with the detective, and her team, was amazing.

She put me in charge of filling her team in on all of my findings before we got to work in putting more of the facts together. It was thrilling, to be leading people and helping them sort through all of the facts they'd already collected.

"Kai, I'm telling you it was amazing."

He chuckles. "I'm glad you enjoyed yourself. Are you any closer to finding a suspect?"

I shake my head as I take a seat in the armchair opposite him. "No, no closer. It's hard to pin it on anyone because of the nature of the attacks. There's no solid pattern other than it happening every two to three days, and that the wounds are the same every time. There's not one individual suspect because quite a lot of the facts point to it, potentially, being more than one person."

"What about your Royal family theory?"

I shrug. "There's not a great deal to go off. We don't know enough of what's going on in the palace. We know nothing of the household staff and there's too many of them to not raise suspicion if we start asking questions. But I do think we can rule the princes out since you can alibi their every move."

He nods, pursing his lips before sipping his beer.

"What?" I question.

"Nothing, nothing," he says, looking away from

me.

"No, it's not nothing. You look guilty. What's going on?"

"There was one night where the princes' snuck out. I didn't know where they'd gone."

"They– they weren't in front of you the whole night?"

He shakes his head. "No, but when they got back in the morning I asked them about it. They said they'd been at the graveyard. That they wanted to say some words to their father and that it couldn't wait."

"Did you believe them?"

"I– I guess–"

"Did you believe them? Yes or no?" I demand.

Stones form in the pit of my stomach at the thought of the princes' being a part of the attacks. The rational part of me knows that they should always be considered as suspects. But the other part of me doesn't want to believe that they could be guilty.

Please don't let them be guilty.

"Yes. Markus gave them an alibi; said he saw them entering and leaving the graveyard that night."

"And do you trust Markus?"

"No. I don't know, I just, the thought has been playing on my mind the last few days."

"Kai, do you think that the princes are behind the attacks?"

He sighs and rubs his chin. "Honestly, no, I don't. But something is going on in that palace, I can tell you that much."

"Do you think I should cancel tomorrow?"

He shakes his head. "They're probably the safest two in the palace right now. Just promise me you'll be careful."

"I promise." I internally cringe at the fact that I've just promised I'll be careful, when I cannot guarantee that the brothers didn't see my tattoos.

"Good."

CHAPTER EIGHT

For 24 hours, I sit and stew in my thoughts.

I can't just forget that Kai *may* have lied to cover up the involvement of the princes, and I can't just forget that they may have seen my tattoos. It's a given they would've looked faded because of the four bracelets I'd put back on, but I've no idea how observant the brothers are in unfamiliar settings.

Despite the worry that has been ebbing under my skin, I haven't worn the bracelets for 24 hours. They began to feel restrictive, and my tattoos were beginning to itch. An itch so deep I thought it was going to drive me mad. But it quickly dissipated once I took the bracelets off. It felt good to have them out in the open, letting the air to them. I even used my talent. I healed a cut on my leg that the cat, who tends to frequent the cottage garden, gave me when I tried to stroke it. It felt good to use the talent, to let my tattoos shimmer and work.

I feel renewed.

I stare at the outfit on my bed. Kai left it on the kitchen table this morning with a note written by Liam. It's the outfit for my date tonight. It's elegant and regal all while simultaneously being simple. A set of soft, flowy trousers with flowers printed all over them and a light, loose fitting crop top made from the same material. It's beautiful.

Everything around me is ready for tonight, yet I don't feel ready. My mind has been fighting itself about my conversation with Kai the other day. I feel extremely conflicted, but the rational part of me knows that nothing has been confirmed, and the main theory the detective and I are running with is that someone is performing blood swaps with the alternate Eilin bloodline, which then allows them to control the infected person.

I stare at the outfit again, wondering if I should start getting ready so that by the time I'm done, hopefully I'll feel like I'm ready. I start by pulling my hair back into two twists, tying them off at the end. Then I pull on underwear and slip into the trousers before lacing up a pair of dainty sandals. I reach for the top at the same time a bang comes from downstairs. I bolt down the stairs, forgetting the top, and burst into the living room to find Kai leaning against the table, bloody and bruised.

"Oh my god," I gasp as I rush to him.

"I'm fine, just– just pull out the chair for me," he groans.

I do as he says, pulling out the head chair at the dining table and helping him sit down.

"Who did this to you?" I ask as I help him peel off his shirt. His torso and back are covered in bruises and slash wounds that are steadily bleeding.

"I don't know. I was coming home to get you, and someone jumped me."

Panic grips me as I check him over, looking for more cuts and injuries. Was Kai meant to be the next victim?

"Did they get you anywhere else?" I ask as I examine the larger cuts.

"No. No, I got a good shot in before I managed to

get awa– Argh, shit. Don't poke them," he groans.

"I need to heal them," I say as I start taking off my bracelets.

"No, no, I'll be fine. You need to get ready," he groans as he tries to get up, but I don't let him. I push on his shoulder, and he sits back down.

I take off the bracelets and wait for my tattoos to appear. Once they've appeared, they start to shimmer as I slowly move my hands over the wounds. I watch as the bleeding stops, and the skin starts to stitch itself back together. I do this for all eight cuts before I work on the bruises. I circle them with one hand and watch as the skin goes back to its normal colour.

"Do you think anything's broken?" I ask as he lets me palpate his stomach before I begin checking his ribs.

He shakes his head. "No. The bruises will be from sparring with the twins this morning."

"You fight the princes?"

"Yeah, sometimes. They're very good, and it gives me the chance to practise as well."

"Kai, those bruises were bad. How hard were you letting the twins hit you? And how often? You're going to do a lot more damage if you don't get everything checked by a doctor, or me."

"It's a new thing, today was the second session. But stop fussing over me," he takes my hands in his, stopping me from assessing him further. "Go and get ready. We'll be late otherwise."

I raise my eyebrows at him. "Just let me finish making sure there's nothing going on internally, then I'll finish changing."

"Fine," he says, rolling his eyes.

I make my assessment quick. Closing my eyes and visualising the inside of the body. I let my talent run over every nerve, muscle, every piece of tissue, organ and vein until I determine that everything is fine.

"You're fine. I'm going to finish dressing, then I'll meet you by the front door."

He nods. "I'm going to have a quick shower and change my clothes. Meet by the door in 10?"

"Sounds good."

I watch as he makes his way to his room, and I listen for the shower before heading upstairs.

CHAPTER NINE

We get to the Rose Arch just as the sun starts to set.

After Kai showered and changed into a less bloody shirt, we quickly made our way to the meeting point.

"It's beautiful," I say, looking around the area.

The Rose Arch is sort of a landmark. It's a beautiful part of a cliff that overlooks the most breathtaking waterfall. Clear, crystal blue water sits below us, tainted with the yellows and reds bleeding down from the sunset. The ground is covered in vibrant and healthy green grass, with rose bushes and hydrangeas surrounding the cliff's edge.

A large building sits off to the left. Stone walls, decaying windows, and moss growing in the cracks. Ivy cascades down one of the stone walls, acting like a privacy curtain, but the faint flickering of orange catches my eye. If I squint hard enough, I think I can make out the shape of a candle in one of the windows.

"Only the best for you, Merry."

I spin round and see Liam first. He's dressed in a black trousers and a black shirt, the sleeves have been rolled up to show off his forearms. A few top buttons have been left unbuttoned. His hair has been gently combed back again and a dimpled smile graces his features. Prince Liam really is a sight to behold.

"You're too kind," I say, smiling as he comes closer.

"Kai, thank you for escorting Meredith here tonight."

"Your welcome, sir. Do you need me for anything else?"

Liam shakes his head. "No, thank you. Go and enjoy the night off."

"Be safe, and enjoy," Kai says to me with a squeeze of my shoulder.

"I will. You be safe also, I'll be home later," I say to him.

"Shall we?" Liam asks, offering me his hand.

"Yes." I take his hand and let him guide me to the stone building.

We carefully walk down the small decline of the grass hill until we reach the front entrance. Liam gestures for me to enter and the first thing that hits me when I step inside is the smokiness of burning candles.

"Vanilla candles?"

"Kai said it was your favourite."

I almost swoon at the thoughtfulness of them asking Kai about my favourite candle. Liam takes my hand and guides me up the grand stone staircase. He chats about when the building was built, when it was abandoned, and when it was bought by the palace to stop the few elected officials from tearing it down.

When we step onto the top floor, he gives me a brief tour of the layout. He lets me read the golden plaques of information that have hung on the walls. He adds a little bit of his own knowledge to the tour which I enjoy a lot. He finishes the tour with a viewing of the old bedrooms which were transformed into rooms for practising old magic.

"Old magic? Why?"

"My family used this place once upon a time, that's why they worked so hard to save it from demolition."

I frown. The records say they saved this place for historical value, for the fact of it being used heavily by the Eilin line. It is a crucial piece of the island's history.

"What do you mean they used it?"

"Rituals. Bloodletting."

My body freezes and my heart skips a beat as Liam pulls me into the room that would've been the ballroom. My blood runs cold as I stare at the altar. Flashes of the books I've read about the rituals used on my ancestors fill my mind. An altar was used in those rituals, and it would've been engraved with the incantations needed for a successful harvest. The symbols and markings helped to cleanse the blood so that it was prepared for the mixing process afterwards.

I sprint for the door but Brandon steps out from thin air and grabs me around the waist. I scream and try to get out of his grasp, pushing at his shoulders and trying to kick him in the hopes that he'll let go. But it's like he's like a wall of stone, completely unmoving as I try to fight him off. I try to hit him in the face, and by some stroke of luck, my fist catches him on the cheek. He briefly lets go, but only so that he can reposition his hands. His hands grip my upper arms as he turns me around and holds me against him, rendering me completely still.

Liam steps closer. I don't stop trying to fight my way out of his hold. I thrash and try to dislodge Brandon's death grip while kicking out my legs at Liam. Unfortunately, he stands just far enough away that my attempts don't reach him.

"Merry, this would go a lot smoother if you stopped fighting us. Just *relax*," he orders, and my body takes on his words. My body immediately stops trying to fight Brandon. Only my mind is still trying to fight, it's racing a million miles a minute as I try to figure out how I'm going to get out of here.

"How did you do that?"

"A little gift from our ancestors," Liam says.

He grabs one of my hands, bringing it up and then encircling my wrist.

"These are very pretty. And expensive. Where did Kai find these?"

"I don't know, he didn't tell me," I rush out, the panic I was trying hard to supress beginning to climb up my throat. "What are you going to do to me?"

He presses a finger to my lips, stopping me from talking.

"Uh, uh. One step at a time," he says as he yanks the bracelets off both of my wrists. The Beads scatter to the floor, bouncing a few times before they roll away. My tattoos start to burn as they reappear.

My bracelets.

"What are you going to do to me?" I ask again.

"We know what you are, Merry. An Eilin with the power to heal, a line that's meant to be extinct."

"No. No, I'm not."

"You are. We saw you heal your brother," Brandon mutters into my ear.

"How? I– Did you–" I cut myself off. Realisation dawns on me, it creeps up my spine and forces its way up my throat.

"Did you have Kai attacked?"

CHAPTER TEN

Liam sighs and nods his head.

My heart drops to the bottom of my stomach at the thought of Brandon and Liam attacking Kai, a man who has been loyal to them for years. Tears burn in my eyes at the thoughts of the two gentle princes' that I met before. The two princes that danced with me at the Ball and made me laugh. Now those are being replaced with the thoughts of them using me for my blood. Of them being able to control me and use me for their own personal gain.

"We had to make sure you were an Eilin. Especially after we saw your faded tattoos at the detective's station. Couldn't just bring you here and be wrong, that wouldn't bode well for nurturing a new relationship."

"What are you going to do to me?" I beg as tears stream down my face.

Brandon presses his cheek against the side of my head. "You are going to be ours. Ours to control, ours to use. You will be our judge, jury and executioner. When we are crowned Kings, you will be our right hand. You will serve us, and you will enact punishments unto those we deem worthy of them."

I shake my head and I begin to try and move, shaking and thrashing as I try to get loose.

"And after this, we're going to marry you so that you are protected by the crown. You will be our equal in public, and our weapon in private."

"No. No, I won't do it. I won't be your personal weapon *or* your wife. Let me go, please. Just let me go," I sob as I try to get out of Brandon's grip.

"That's the problem, sweetheart, you don't have a choice," Liam says, and I feel Brandon press his lips to the side of my head.

I bend at the knees as he tries to pull me toward the altar, trying to turn myself into a deadweight, but Liam doesn't let that slide. He steps forward and waits as Brandon pulls me back up, ensuring that I place my feet flat on the floor. Liam grasps my chin in his hand.

"You *will* lay on the altar and not move unless I tell you to," he orders, using his Control on me.

My body takes it. It lets Brandon pick me up bridal style and place me on my back in the middle of the altar.

Brandon moves my arms and legs so that I'm lying in a star position. I can't see either brother, so I just stare at the ceiling, wishing to be somewhere else. Wishing that Kai didn't leave me earlier because he trusts the princes. Wishing that I could go back in time and insist that I wanted Kai to stay with us. Tell them that I wasn't feeling safe because of the attacks. I should've known that the Royal family played a part in this mess, I should've known that Brandon and Liam were involved in this. I shouldn't have been an idiot and trusted them.

I close my eyes, holding back the tears. I can't give my tears to these princes; they don't deserve them.

"Oh, sweetheart, you *need* to keep your eyes open for this," Liam says, patting my cheek tenderly. The action makes the tears I was trying so hard not to let fall start to flow down my face. "Don't cry. This will all be over soon, and then we'll go to the church, and we'll get married. You'll wear a pretty dress; we'll say our vows and then we'll show you your new home."

I shake my head and let the tears fall as Brandon comes back into view. He smiles down at me before lifting up a blade. *A jade blade.* I whimper and pull my face to the side, but Liam doesn't let that slide. He gently braces his hands on either side of my face, moving my gaze so that I'm looking back up at the ceiling.

Brandon moves out of my eyesight again, and the only way I know where he has gone is by the gentle touch to my wrist. He rolls up the sleeves of the top I'm wearing before he lifts my arm up at an angle and places my palm facing up to the ceiling. Instinctually, I tense my hand into a fist, but Liam is quick to fix it by ordering me to relax my entire body. He keeps a close eye on me, his gorgeous brown eyes– I hate that they're so pretty– bore down into mine.

I feel the cold tip of the blade touch the middle of my arm, just under the crease of my elbow. He presses the blade into my skin, and I feel the burn as he pulls the blade down, stopping just before my wrist. He places my wrist back down; the wound being placed directly over one of the hollow engravings. Brandon then does the same thing to my left wrist before walking away.

Liam's eyes don't leave mine at all, not even when mine start to close from the dizziness taking over. My body feels heavy and my arms sting as they bleed.

"Plea–please."

"It's okay. You're okay, Merry," Brandon says as he comes back into view. "Liam's going to stitch you back up while I give you a blood replacer."

A chill runs through my body as I close my eyes, letting the dizziness temporarily fry my brain.

※

My eyes flutter open as the dizziness begins to fade.

I look up at the ceiling and remember what I'm doing here. I try to move, shuffling myself around on the altar as I try to find a good, and comfortable, position in which to try and sit up. I try to use my arms, but the skin feels like it's being ripped apart. I groan in pain and look down. I see that the wounds have been stitched up and covered with a clear, medical wrapping.

"You're awake," Liam says as he comes to stand in front of me. I swing my legs over the side of the altar and Liam instantly helps me up. One arm wraps around my waist, pulling me close so that I'm leaning against his chest. The dizziness returns, closely followed by nausea.

"Liam, shall I show our *wife* what we did with her blood while she was sleeping?" Brandon asks, and I glare at him for the use of the title *wife*.

"That sounds like a very good idea," Liam agrees as Brandon walks over to the other side of the altar.

"You see, Merry," Liam starts. "Your blood was mixed with the natural cleansing agent from the altar. We mixed the clean blood with the chemicals you saw set up earlier. It was then injected into my veins."

"Wha– what does that mean?" I ask weakly. I struggle to keep my head up and end up, unwillingly, leaning my temple against Liam's chest.

"I can now control you fully. Your mind, body and soul are mine," Liam clarifies as he tightens his hold on me. One of his hands comes up to my face and moves my gaze so that it's focused on Brandon.

Brandon flashes a needle, the syringe full of what I assume to be my blood. He gives me a smile before carefully sticking the needle into his arm. He empties the plunger. His eyelids flutter open and shut as his eyes roll to the back of his head. He lets the needle fall to the floor as the mini convulsions slow down. It takes him a second, his gaze glassy and far away from here. When he fully comes back to himself, he walks around the altar so that he's standing in front of me.

"See that. Your blood is slowly combining with mine and then we'll be complete. A proper unit, a *family*," he says as he points to the silver track marks making their way up.

Liam manoeuvres me so that I have my back pressed to his front. Brandon steps forward, caging me in. His hands come up and cup my face before he lowers his own face down to mine. His nose brushes mine and I close my eyes. The drowsiness takes over and I let my face just relax into his hold. I know fighting it is useless, my body and mind are no longer mine to control.

'Cos This Is How Villains Are Made

"Detective Turner, please come in here," Liam calls.

I hear faint footsteps against the wooden floor. Brandon lets up his grip on my face and I manage to turn my head. Detective Turner walks in with Meika in tow. I feel my control come back as I catch sight of Meika's predicament. She's been handcuffed, her hands behind her back. She's got a rag tied across her mouth and tears are streaming down her face.

"Meika," I wheeze.

"You see, rumours travel fast round this island. And rumours within the palace of a strange package being snuck in inside of a crate of *kilchanca*. Witnesses say they saw Meika collect said package and give it to Kai," Brandon says as Liam lets go of me. Brandon pulls me to his chest and tilts my head up.

I scrunch my face up.

"It took us a while to figure everything out. Trying to get hold of the chain of custody was difficult, no one was willing to talk. But upon asking Detective Turner to look into it for us, we found that Kai had the Beads brought in by a merchant. A merchant who deals with other worldly items and olden artefacts. Did you know that Blocking Beads are considered an artefact now?" Liam continues.

"You two are sick," Meika shouts, clearly having spat out the gag.

"Is that why you ran, Meika? Because you think we're sick? Or is it because you were going to tell people about what we've been doing?" Brandon asks this time.

"You had me researching bloodlines and rituals and then you locked me in a room. Do you know what they did then, Merry?"

I shake my head.

"They stuck a needle in me and started taking my blood. They noticed the scar-like tattoos along my collarbone and around my wrists. They took my blood and started using it to get innocent people to murder other innocent people."

"You're an Eilin?" I ask as I manage to get out of Brandon's grip. Strangely, he lets me walk over to Meika without interfering.

"Not Eilin. *Aeylin*. The anti-blood, the poisoners favourite. Your princes knew that there was an Eilin

'Cos This Is How Villains Are Made

on the island, but they didn't know where. All they had was Kai being the one to pick up the package. Then you waltzed into the palace gardens for one of your many lunch dates, with your smiles, and your bracelets. They instantly knew it was you, they just had to visually confirm it."

I swallow thickly.

"What will happen to Kai?" I ask, turning to Liam.

"Nothing, as long as he agrees with our union. And if you want him to remain safe and alive then you'll keep your mouth shut about what happened here," Liam tells me. I feel the control working and all I can do is nod.

"Good girl," he says as one of his hands comes to rest gently on the back of my neck. "Now, while Brandon deals with Meika, there's–"

"What's going to happen to Meika?" I ask worriedly, interrupting him.

"That is the one and only time I will allow you to interrupt me, do you understand?" he questions with a deadly tone, and I feel his hand that's on the back of my neck tense.

I nod, looking him in the eyes.

"In answer to your question, Brandon is just going to help Meika get a little more comfortable in her role as your Lady-In-Waiting. She'll be there for you every step of your journey as our Queen."

I nod, my mouth feeling as though it's been taped shut. The strong control that Liam has over me is frightening.

"But for now, my darling wife, this is your defining moment. The moment you are going to fulfil your title as our weapon."

I try to say something, but I can't.

"What is it, my love?" Liam asks patronisingly as he tucks a piece of fallen out hair behind my ear.

"What do you mean?" I spit. The words were right on the tip of my tongue, waiting to be let out.

"You need to *dispose* of the Detective. She knows too much."

"What?" I ask despite the compulsion and control he has over me which makes me pull away from him. I reach for the closest blade.

"Merry, our wife." Brandon starts as he steps over to Liam and I. Meika follows close behind him,

pulling Detective Turner alongside her. "We want–
no, need –you to kill Leigh Turner."

I improve my grip on the blade's handle. I twirl it in my hand as I walk over to Turner. While a small part of my mind screams at me to stop this, to disobey his order; the other part tells me to keep going. To do as he says.

I step so that the toes of my shoes touch Turner's. She's begging and pleading and crying but none of that stops me. I pull back the dagger before using as much force as possible and lodge it into her stomach at an upwards angle. She screams as I twist the blade before I pull it back out.

Meika lets Turner fall to her knees before she drops onto her side. She cries out in pain. I stare at her and then at the bloodied blade in my hand. Then I let the tears stream down my face.

"Good job. They say the first is the hardest, but you are strong. You are the Queen. *Our* Queen," Brandon says. He removes the blade from my hand before threading his fingers through mine. He quickly leans down toward Meika, telling her to clean everything up before she's to meet us at the church.

Liam does the same, linking his hand in mine before they both stand in front of me. Shoulder to shoulder as they place my hands over their hearts.

"Our Queen. Our judge, jury, executioner and wife."

"Ours for chaos. Ours for mayhem."

Something inside of me wants to repeat their words, and I can't stop the words as they tumble out of my mouth. "Yours for chaos, for justice and punishment. *Your* Queen."

'Cos This Is How Villains Are Made

ABOUT THE AUTHOR

A. Carys is a self-published author from Portsmouth, United Kingdom. Other than spending 90% of her day writing, she also loves to crochet, read, and take photos of her family's cats.

Printed in Great Britain
by Amazon